Frederic William Farrar

The Paths of Duty

Counsels to Young Men

Frederic William Farrar

The Paths of Duty
Counsels to Young Men

ISBN/EAN: 9783742862662

Manufactured in Europe, USA, Canada, Australia, Japa

Cover: Foto ©Andreas Hilbeck / pixelio.de

Manufactured and distributed by brebook publishing software
(www.brebook.com)

Frederic William Farrar

The Paths of Duty

THE PATHS OF DUTY

Counsels to Young Men

BY

THE VERY REV. F. W. FARRAR, D.D.

DEAN OF CANTERBURY

NINTH THOUSAND

NEW YORK
THOMAS Y. CROWELL & COMPANY
PUBLISHERS

INTRODUCTION.

THESE papers have been written in compliance with a request from the editor of *The Young Man.* The young have the long years of future before them; and all good men, who have themselves begun to enter into the Valley of the Shadow, cannot but look with the deepest interest on those who will be fighting the difficult battle of life, in that warfare which has no discharge, long after they themselves are sleeping with their fathers. I have given to young men, in the simplest and most straightforward manner, the advice which seemed to me most likely to be truly helpful to them. That advice is founded, throughout, upon a somewhat wide and varied experience of life. If, in giving it, I have frequently appealed to the words of others, it is because I wished to bring weightier evidence and testimony than my own to bear upon the precepts which I offered; and if I often quote the words of the poets, it is because I have ever found them to be the deepest, as well as the most delightful, of moral teachers.

May God bless these unpretending pages to the benefit of the young men who read them in America and in Greater Britain, as well as in England.

F. W. FARRAR.

CONTENTS.

		PAGE
INTRODUCTION	. . . .	3
I.	THE YOUNG MAN IN THE HOME	7
II.	THE YOUNG MAN IN BUSINESS	19
III.	THE YOUNG MAN IN THE CHURCH	32
IV.	THE YOUNG MAN AND MARRIAGE	45
V.	THE YOUNG MAN MASTER OF HIMSELF	59

Google

THE PATHS OF DUTY.

I.

THE YOUNG MAN IN THE HOME.

It happens frequently that a young man, after an interval of years, finds himself once more, for a time, in the old home of his childhood. He has gone to school as a young boy, and then only his holidays were spent at home. But after his school or college days are over, it is often his destiny to reside under the old roof, during the earlier part of his career, either in his father's business, or in some one of the many occupations provided by great cities. Now, this renewal of the old home-life, under changed conditions, may be either very delightful, both to himself and to all his family, or it may be intolerably irksome.

It will be delightful if, having learnt unselfishness and self-control, the youth brings back with him not only his mature strength and healthy frame, but also the flower of all the best morality which he has learnt from parents, teachers, and companions.

It will be intolerable if he has not learnt the meaning of the lesson that no man liveth and no man dieth unto himself; and that the life of egotism and self-indulgence, though it has its root in pride and vanity, is worthy only of the animal, not of the man with the dignity of God's image upon him, and the sign of his redemption marked visibly upon his forehead. In the bearing of the young man in his home, there may be an exhibition of all fair humanities — of all that is courteous, pure, lovely, and of good report — of true manliness and beautiful chivalry; or, on the other hand, an offensive display of paltry animalism and odious ingratitude.

Concrete and real examples may, perhaps, give more definiteness to what I have to impress.

But first I must pause to say a word to parents. They cannot be reminded too often, or too earnestly, not to fret, not to *worry* their children. That may sound like very homely advice; yet it has been thought worthy of a place on the sacred page by the Apostle of the Gentiles. The clause, καὶ οἱ πατέρες μὴ ἐρεθίζετε τὰ τέκνα ὑμῶν, rendered in our A.V., "and ye fathers, provoke not your children to wrath," means exactly, "do not *irritate* your children," "do not rub them up the wrong way." Parents must respect their children as well as children their parents. The whole sacredness of humanity lies in every human being; and it involves an independent individuality, a separate development. Our children are not, and cannot be, either pale or brilliant reflexes of ourselves. They have separate wills; they are new and peculiar entities; a whole eternity lies in them; the soul of each of them is an island, and it is surrounded by an unvoyageable sea. We must recognize their separateness, and not try to cramp the forming crystal into an impossible mould, which would but flaw and ruin it.

Obedience and love from their children are the happy due of all parents who have faithfully done their duty; but the nature and the limits of the respect alter with

the advancing years. There is such a thing as the un-
natural repression of grown-up children by their parents, and the continuance of unfair demands upon their
loyalty. And in the case of young men we have especially to remember the ebullient life which for us has
long passed away. We have to make allowance for the
faults and tendencies which are as inherent in youth as
they are in childhood. " Young men," says Lord Bacon,
" in their conduct and management of actions, embrace
more than they can hold; stir more than they quiet; fly
to the end, without consideration of the means and
degrees; pursue some few principles which they have
chanced upon absurdly; use extreme remedies at first,
and, that which doubleth all errors, will not acknowl-
edge or retract them." Over young men, therefore, we
must aim to establish a wise influence, rather than a
galling control; and, without too obtrusive a resort to
didactics, we must lead them to feel the force of the
warning of Ecclesiastes : " Rejoice, O young man, in
thy youth, and let thy heart cheer thee in the days
of thy youth; and walk in the ways of thy heart, and
in the light of thine eyes : but remember " — and this
memento is uttered rather in the spirit of genial kind-
ness than of unsympathizing menace — " but remember
that for all these things God shall bring thee into judgment."

Here, then, are specimens of some " young men at
home," — faithful and unfaithful, obedient and disobe-
dient, happy and unhappy, wise and unwise.

1. I recall three who were, in succession, young men
in the same home. One was training to be a doctor;
the second to be a civil servant; the third to be a
clergyman. The home was sufficiently comfortable and

well-to-do, but simple. It was so occupied with the round of incessant duties as to leave less room than might be desirable for the graces and innocent amusements of society. Yet each of those youths in succession resigned the games and cheerful society of boyish life; fell quietly into the home routine. They worked heartily in their own rooms; made themselves bright, happy, and contented; tried faithfully to prepare themselves for the battle of life, and the struggle to earn a living; and never gave their parents an hour's anxiety by unreasonable demands, or extravagance, or dubious pleasures, or even by that reserve and reticence respecting their aims, pursuits, and friendships which may sometimes create heartburn and misgiving even where there is no reasonable ground for it. And so they passed away to life, or early death, leaving behind them good hopes and happy memories; they left their homes to become "profitable members of the church and commonwealth," and hereafter, we hope, "partakers of the immortal glories of the Resurrection."

2. I recall another young man in his home — a very great and famous man whose name I must not mention. His was the case of a man of genius, born of parents who had no pretensions to genius at all, and who was incomparably in advance of his parents in culture and education. Many a young man so circumstanced has been tempted to give himself airs; to look down upon his parents as inferiors; to shudder when they drop their *h's;* to condole with himself as the offspring of bourgeois or plebeian people, of whom he is obliged to be ashamed. Not so the young man of whom I speak. He had taken as his rule of life the highest of all ideals, — the ideal of Him "who went down to his parents at Nazareth, and

was subject unto them." I have sat at his table, and heard him pour forth the stores of his unexampled eloquence, and unroll the treasures of his large heart, in lessons full of depth and beauty; and then his dear old mother — a perfect type of English middle-class womanhood, with something of the holy Philistinism of a narrow creed which invests its humblest votaries with self-imagined infallibility — would lift up her monitory finger before the assembled guests and say, "Now, William," — we will call him "William," though that was not his name, — "listen to me." Then, while he and we respectfully listened, she would lay down the law with exquisite placidity, telling him how completely mistaken he was in these new-fangled notions: —

> " Proving all wrong that hitherto was writ,
> And putting us to ignorance again."

"Yes, mother," he would say when her little admonition ended; and then conversation would resume its flow quite undisturbed, and the dear old lady was more than satisfied. It was the *greatness* of her son's genius which made him so good a son. A smaller mind would have winced, or been contemptuous. "Men do not make their homes unhappy because they have genius," says Wordsworth, "but because they have *not enough genius;* a mind and sentiment of a higher order would render them capable of seeing and feeling all the beauty of domestic ties."

3. Another young man in his home! He was at college, and had several young brothers at Eton, or preparing for Eton. He was not at all a saint, but he was a gentleman; and the one element which helped to make his life useful and honorable was his sense of duty

towards his home. One day the brothers were sitting
together, and no one with, them but another young
Trinity man, when one of the lads made use of a coarse
word to a younger brother. Instantly the elder brother
started up, and, without saying a word, gave the boy a
sound box on the ears, and turned him, then and there,
out of the room. I am quite sure that the young
Etonian learnt a lesson for life. He learnt that respect was due to his younger as well as to his elder
brothers ; and that, if ever he could sink so low as to
use coarse language, at any rate he should *not* do it in
his father's house.

4. Now, in this instance we see one great sphere of
influence which a young man may exercise in his home.
He may be of the greatest use to his sisters by enabling
them really to estimate the worth or the worthlessness
of the young men who visit the home, and who may
aspire to be their husbands; but he may be of *incalcu-
lable* use to his younger brothers. He has seen more
of life than they have. They naturally look up to him
for their views as to what things are, or are not, to be
desired ; what things should or should not be pursued.
I have known elder brothers who were a source of blessing and inspiration, and others who were a downright
curse, to the younger members of their family.

5. I think the elder brother of the Prodigal must
have been a specimen of the latter class, — not, indeed,
by any directly perverting influence, but negatively, by
the selfishness which was incapable of forbearance and
sympathy. Absorbed in his own laborious virtues, he
despised the young ne'er-do-weel, his brother, and let
him take his own line, without troubling himself to
guide or love. But for him, and his hard immaculate-

ness, unsociability, and lack of love, the Prodigal might never have become a prodigal; and since he had no love for any one but his estimable self, it is no wonder that when the poor youth came back, hungry, degraded, and in rags, the elder brother, so far from sharing in his father's joy over the son who had been dead and was alive again, who had been lost and was found, had nothing for the occasion but unforgiving jealousy, cold sneers, and harsh exaggerations. Such young men are an alien influence in the homes where they abide.

And what a fatal loss they suffer! For, as Mr. W. H. Mallock says, " A man's home, his family, his means of livelihood, — these are the chalice which holds the sacramental wine of his life; and if we allow the chalice to be soiled or leaky, the wine will be defiled or wasted. God wills that it should not be wasted. . . . If we are responsible when we make our brother to offend, are we not equally responsible if we make him to offend by leaving him in conditions where nothing but offence is possible ? "

6. But I know an elder brother very different from this, who has been an inestimable blessing to all of his family. He and they were left orphans; and there were several young boys, as well as the girls, who had to be started in life. Without a murmur, in complete self-sacrifice of his own hopes and his own interests, this young man undertook the entire responsibility of his family. He gave up all present thoughts of marrying, or surrounding himself with the comforts and pleasures which might otherwise have been in his power. He regarded the younger orphans as his sacred charge, and even now is toiling on to supply them with the means and the opportunities of which they had been deprived

by the loss of their parents. How invaluable is the work of such a young man in his home! how high the reward which his unselfishness should earn, when his brothers and sisters rise up and call him blessed! "The essence of greatness," says Emerson, "is the perception that virtue is enough." "If the home duties be well performed," so wrote Confucius some twenty-five hundred years ago, "there is no need to go afar to offer sacrifice."

7. The experience of life brings before us, alas! bad examples as well as good. I recall young men whose inconsiderateness and misconduct made home unendurable alike to their families and to themselves. They *would* have their latchkeys; they *would* stay out to any hour they liked; even if they were engaged in things not necessarily harmful, and with friends not necessarily pernicious, they would not deign to share their thoughts or their proceedings with the home circle, and did not greatly care if they surmised the worst. Their silence was more cruel than bitter words. I have known such a state of things end in the abomination of mutual quarrels, and even of deplorable scenes, between sons and fathers, until it became impossible for them to live at all under the same roof. The prodigals went their way, perhaps to lose all and forfeit everything, and to end by earning scant and laborious livelihoods under harder conditions than those of the ordinary English laborer, and with barely, perhaps, even the prospect of a workhouse at the close. I have known them make miserable marriages, squander their inheritance, and shatter every high hope which had once been formed for them. I have known them come back from the antipodes, wretched and penniless, and yet walk again

and again before the door of their parents, afraid and ashamed to knock or to lift the latch, not knowing what welcome would await them, afraid even that they might be altogether and deservedly repulsed. And the most frightful cases of all have been the cases of young men left in the homes of widowed mothers. What can a poor widowed mother, struggling for bare existence, do with sons who, living under her roof, choose to be wild and unruly? She may have been a good mother; but if her sons are not to be controlled or coerced by the indefeasible sacredness of motherhood,— if they forsake the guide of their youth, and forget the covenant of their God,—if in the twilight, in the evening, in the black and dark night, they will go as oxen to the slaughter, and as fools to the correction of the stocks, till a dart strike through their own liver,— what can the poor helpless mother do, perhaps heartbroken and sick, and struggling, and vainly trying, it may be, to prevent the daughters also from following the revolt of the sons?— what can she do in her helplessness, in her widowhood, under the hard conditions of her life?— what can she do in that most pathetic of all lots, but uplift to heaven her appealing hands and tear-dimmed eyes, and—

> ". . . fall with all her weight of cares
> Upon the world's great altar-stairs
> That slope through darkness up to God"?

Oh if, of those who read these pages, there should be but one young man whose conscience shall here start up before him with menacing finger and outstretched hand, and say to him in that still, small voice which is louder than the thunders of Sinai, "*Thou art the man!*" let him for very shame amend his ways! For meta-

phorically as it may be expressed by Eastern imagination, there is yet a stern truth in the saying, — so
heinous in God's sight is the sin of ingratitude and
unfilial disloyalty to parents, — "The eye that mocketh
at his father or his mother, and despiseth to obey, the
ravens of the valley shall pick it out, and the young
eagles shall eat it."

8. There is, then, ample verge and room enough for
noble life to every young man in his home. The foe to
the accomplishment of these aims is the inveterate pride
and self-assertiveness of our nature, the rank and flaunt-
ing weed which is the Devil's favorite flower, because
he well knows that its poisonous seeds are prolific and
multiform. This green gay hemlock of the spring with-
ers into dead and unsightly stalks full of cold and
benumbing poison. The longer I live the more it seems
to me that *Humility* is the most characteristic of all the
Christian graces. It is the root of that love which is
the very bond of peace and of all virtues. When once
a young man has learnt that life is service — that it is
not *he* who turns the crank of the universe! — that he,
like every one of us, is in himself profoundly insignificant, and that in this —

"Endless trouble of ants mid a million million of suns,"

our sole importance springs, not from ourselves, but
from conformity to the will of God, and union with our
fellow-men; when once he has learnt that the true
significance of life lies in service rendered to our brethren, as the outcome of love and obedience to God —
when he has thoroughly learnt this, he cannot easily
blind himself with clay.

The warning which might be addressed to hundreds

of young men is, " Ye think too much of yourselves, ye
sons of Levi !" And this is what gives such value to
the advice of Henry Ward Beecher : " Let me say to
every one that is beginning life — Do not begin with
exaggerated ideas of your own worth. Do not think
that you, without battle, ought to be the victor, and
walk from the beginning with those laurels about your
head which are to be twined there, if at all, only at the
end of the campaign. Do not mistake your own tur-
bulent pride, your own false-interpreting, lying vanity.
Do not begin your life fancying that such a fine young
fellow as you are, one so spruce, so handsome, so well
dressed, so accomplished in various way, deserves a
high place. Do not flatter yourself that life owes you
more than it owes anybody else. It owes you, in common with all others, just as much as, climbing, you can
bring down. It owes you a chance to be something.
It will give you that and nothing more."

Many young men, like many young women, act like
caged birds beating their wings to pieces against what
they regard as their too narrow cage, and longing to
wing their way into the boundless blue. Rightly regarded, their cage may be to them a universe, which
shall give large scope for their best and highest facul-
ties. We may give them the excellent advice which
Carlyle wrote to such a young lady in 1866 : " Were
your duties never so small, I advise you set yourself
with double and treble energy to do them, hour after
hour, day after day, in spite of the devil's teeth ! What
is our answer to all inward devils ? — ' This I *can* do, O
devil, and I do it, thou seest, in the name of God.'
Were it but the more perfect regulation of your apart-
ments, the sorting away of your clothes, the arranging

of your papers, 'whatsoever thy hand findeth to do, do it with thy might' and all thy worth and constancy. *Much more if your duties are of evidently higher, wider scope; if you have brothers, sisters, a father, a mother, weigh earnestly what claim does lie upon you on behalf of each, and consider it as the one thing needful to pay them more and more honestly and nobly what you owe.* What matter how miserable one is if one can do that?"

II.

THE YOUNG MAN IN BUSINESS.

THE commerce of England, which has spread with
unprecedented rapidity and enormous increase of vol-
ume during the present century, is one of the most
visible signs of her wealth, and one of the main sources
of her greatness and influence in the world. "The
white wake of the Atlantic vessels," said Emerson, "is
the true avenue to the palace-front of this seafaring
people." The white sails of our merchant vessels are
dotted over every sea; and there is hardly an islet-rock
in the remote Pacific, or the desolate Antarctic Circle,
which has not seen the black smoke-flag of our steamers.
We have turned the expansive vapor into our giant and
all-powerful slave. We have seized the lightning by
its wings of flame, and bidden it obediently to flash our
humblest messages round the girdled globe, through
tunnelled mountains and the abysses of stormy seas.
God has made us the accumulators of the world's riches,
the carriers of its burdens, the manufacturers of its
most universal goods. Yet splendid and immense as is
the domain of our world-empire, which makes us the
possessors of one-sixth of the land surface of the globe,
such prosperity and power have in them no elements of
inherent permanence. "Assyria, Greece, Rome, Car-
thage, — where are they?" What Lord Beaconsfield
said was not only eloquent, but true: that though we
were greater than Venice or than Tyre, yet if we were

not faithful to our high mission as a nation, our glory might fade like the Tyrian dyes, and crumble like the Venetian palaces.

It is a necessary consequence of our commercial greatness that vast multitudes of our young men earn their living in business, and that a large part of this "business" is directly or indirectly commercial. What the young men now are in their business character and relations, that will the future of England be.

In the old warrior commonwealths of Greece, fine muscular development, perfect physical beauty, heroic and self-sacrificing courage in the battlefield, were held to be of the supremest importance. They would have hailed the spirit of the verse of our modern poet: —

> "Vain mightiest fleets of iron framed,
> Vain those all-conquering guns,
> Unless proud England keep untamed
> The true heart of her sons."

Nothing can better illustrate the consummate importance which they attached to their young men, than the old Doric annual procession, in which the male population walked in three divisions: first, those who were past the zenith of their life; then those who were in the full flush of youth; lastly, the boys. Each, as they marched along, sang an iambic line. The elders sang: —

> "In former days we lived as stalwart youths."

The young men sang: —

> "Strong youths we are; and try us if thou wilt.'

Then the boys, with all the confidence of boyish audacity, sang: —

> "Ay, and we shall be! better far than both."

The Greeks thus showed that to them the best meaning and value of life was crowded into those flushed and fleeting years, when youth danceth like a bubble, nimble and gay, and shineth like a dove's neck or the lustre of a rainbow, which hath no substance, but of which the very image and colors are fantastical.

Now, physical health and vigor will never cease to be of capital importance for the youth of any nation which would not "lose the wrestling thews which throw the world." If we ever sink into a nationally puny physique, it is probable that we may become at the same time slight-natured and miserable. But of this, in the middle and upper classes, there is no danger. At any school in the kingdom we may see "our young barbarians all at play," and may agree with Wellington, when looking at the playing-fields of Eton, he exclaimed, "It was there that Waterloo was won!" Cricket, football, tennis, golf, bicycling, rowing, athletic sports, gymnastic contests, have rendered a real service to the health and strength of all the youth of the English people, even in our great overcrowded cities, and will continue to do so, unless they get corroded with the dry-rot of betting. There is more danger of athletics being made *too* prominent than of their falling into neglect. Certainly we would advise every youth to promote sanity of mind by health of body, and to remember that "you cannot rumple the jerkin without rumpling the jerkin's lining." We will assume, then, that the young man begins his business career with a strong and healthy frame; and we would advise him, even on moral grounds, to cultivate strength and health to the best of his power, as a means of furthering the usefulness as well as the happiness of his life.

But many other things are of supreme importance, and it is by moral qualities that the young man who aims at a high ideal in business must make his mark.

1. For instance, it is almost superfluous to dwell on the necessity for *inflexible honesty and integrity.* It is, I suppose, sometimes possible for an individual to make a sudden fortune by fraud and wrong; and it seems to be possible to make a fortune by an unblushing and blatant puffing, which is a vulgar and greedy element in modern life. But such means of enrichment are of their very nature extremely fugitive, and no nation's commerce could subsist by them uninjured for a single decade. The foundation of English commerce, at any rate till comparatively recent times, was its thoroughness and soundness. All our customers throughout the world could rely on English goods. They were what they pretended to be. There were no shams or shoddy in them. Whether this continues to be the case so universally as of old I do not know; but certain it is that every young man's influence should be used to further rigid integrity. George Eliot, in " Middlemarch," was drawing a picture from the life when she described the gradual and disastrous collapse of Mr. Vincy's prosperity from the time when he began to use the cheap dyes recommended by his sham-religious brother-in-law, which were soon found to rot the silks for which he had once been famous.

Those who have examined English commerce, and profess to know its secrets, do not hesitate to declare that it involves a large amount of adulteration; and no less a writer than Mr. Herbert Spencer, in a celebrated paper on English trade, pointed to the existence of many methods and practices to which, if they really exist, no other name than that of chicanery and dishonesty can be applied. That the young man in business may chance to be brought into contact with concerns conducted in a manner which will not stand the test — that he may find himself in positions in which it is assumed that he will not shrink from telling half-truths which are nearly akin to falsehood — that he may find himself initiated into certain secrets of the prison-house, unknown to the general public, which, to a sensitive conscience, seem tainted with imposture — is certain. I have not unfrequently received letters from young men who have found themselves placed in circumstances which caused them a constant struggle with the reproofs of a troubled conscience ; and from others who, unable to sell their souls either for a mess of pottage or for a livelihood, have thrown up their situations, and faced the terrible difficulties of finding fresh employment rather than do what no sophistry could persuade them to regard as fair or even excusable. It seems hard to advise a young man so circumstanced to take the manly and courageous course, — to do the right, and at all costs to shame the Devil. One who has never been called upon to make so serious a sacrifice may almost shrink from the cheap and easy task of telling another that *he* ought to make it. Yet if God be God, if the supereminent beatitude of right-doing have all the certainty of a law, there ought to be no possible hesitation about the matter. To face even the abandonment of a situation, on grounds of scrupulous honesty, may seem, in some cases, a terrible sacrifice to make ; but " what shall it profit a man if he gain the whole world, and lose his own soul ? "

2. Next I would mention *diligence and a certain disin-*

terested devotion to his employers' service as an essential for the highest success of the young man in business. A very rich man, who died with a title, once said to me, "Because I have been successful in life many young men come to me and ask me to give them a start. But they all want to begin more or less where and how I *end,* not where and how I *began.* My own history was this: I was the son of poor parents; the only education I ever got was at a free school, which I left at the age of fourteen. I was then put into an office. I did my very best there; but, as I was determined to get on, I looked out for the most eminent man in my profession, went to him, and asked him to let me work for him gratuitously when my business hours were over, simply that I might thoroughly understand the conditions of the business to which I had been apprenticed. He allowed me to come and work in the evening in his office, with no salary. I worked hard. By the end of the year I had learnt what I wished, but I had also made myself indispensable; and the great man pressed me to enter his service with a good and increasing salary. That was the foundation of my present fortune. . . . Yes," he continued, "there is a checque for a hundred pounds for your church. Don't thank me! I really shall not miss it in the slightest degree at the end of the year. It makes no difference to me."

His remarks were only an illustration of the proverb that the crowd is all at the bottom. "There's plenty of room at the top."

3. The conduct of this youth was mainly "wisdom for a man's self;" but while it is the surest rule for success that a youth should make himself indispensable, he may be assured that, in nine cases out of ten, in pro-

moting the interests of his employer he is promoting his own. In the world of clerkdom, which is a very crowded world, our young Englishmen often murmur that, in many great regions of commerce, they are being ousted by German clerks. But why is this? The best things go to those who are best prepared for them. Another very wealthy man of high station, and a member of Parliament, told me that if he advertised for a clerk who knew enough of modern languages to conduct a wide business correspondence, he could over and over again find German youths. They had come to England and served for nothing in order to learn English, and, while they were content with modest salaries, could often speak and write three or four languages, whereas the English candidates rarely knew anything but English. Naturally, he was obliged to engage those whose knowledge made them most serviceable.

4. He also mentioned a remarkable trait of difference between his German and his English clerks. When six o'clock came, and the business hours were over, every English clerk would jump up from his seat the moment the clock struck, shut his books with a bang, hurry them into his desk, and be off in a moment to his gymnasium and his bicycle. The German clerks would, in the interests of their employer and his business, quietly wait till they had finished the particular matter on which they were occupied. All our sympathies may be with the English lads; but it is obvious that the others would be more likely to get promoted, and to earn higher salaries.

5. The rise of this gentleman himself from the humblest of poor and humble homes to be a county member and the head of a great industry, was due entirely to

energetic promptness. A cargo had been consigned to a dubious foreign company. There might yet be time to prevent its being handed over, if some one would take the journey of five or six hundred miles. The employers summoned their confidential clerks, and asked them whether they would undertake this difficult matter, and when they would start. Some of them said they would try, and would be ready to start the next day. This young man said, "I am ready now. I will start at once." The firm without hesitation intrusted the task to him. He started that evening, travelled night and day, without stopping to sleep, or even to change his clothes; arrived just in time; prevented the unpacking of the cargo, and saved his employers thousands of pounds. So great was the service which he had rendered, that, on his return, he was promoted to the position of a junior partner. He had become the chief acting partner before he attained to middle life, and is now a man of rank and importance. "Seest thou the man diligent in his business? he shall stand before kings, he shall not stand before mean men."

6. But the young man in business, if he is living a much more ideal life than that which keeps a too exclusive eye on the main chance; if, in the demands of business, he does not forget the loftier and more eternal claims of a noble human life, — must cultivate also *a certain courage and independence of manly rectitude.* Whatever may be his business, he will be thrown among others of his own age; and it is one of his highest duties, not only to abstain from setting a bad and dangerous example, but also to escape the average, and to maintain a high standard before all men. And this is where the fear of man, the feebleness which is afraid to

say "No," makes so many young men fail. When Benjamin Franklin was a youth in a printing-office, the other lads went out to bring in for lunch their foaming tankards of beer or porter. Franklin was then a total abstainer from conviction, which was very rare in those days. His comrades laughed at him, and jeered him to their hearts' content, as a milksop and a fool; but he held his own with unwavering good-humor. All those other printers' lads died in humble obscurity, but Franklin rose to greatness and immortality.

"Eripuit coelo fulmen, sceptrumque tyrannis."

In the courageous steadfastness of his boyish character, we see one of the secrets of his future eminence.

7. The quality is needed wherever men, and, above all, wherever young men, are gathered together. It is needed in the army, both among officers and privates. Cromwell's Ironsides went to battle each with a Bible in his knapsack, and were sneered at as snuffling and hypocritical " saints," — strange that the word descriptive of the grandest of human characters should be regarded by the coarsely vulgar as the bitterest of sneers ! — but they made the Cavalier chivalry skip. Nelson's "Methodists" were the most trusted of his crews. Havelock's "Saints" saved India. Once in Burmah, when nearly every other soldier was drunk, and the enemy threatened a most dangerous surprise, the general was in great anxiety and alarm. But one of his officers said to him, "Send for Havelock's ' Saints ; ' his men are never drunk, and Havelock is always ready." But undoubtedly such faithfulness of high principle costs something, especially at first. A youth in my parish enlisted. He was a total abstainer, and a

splendid young fellow. He rapidly rose to be a ser geant. The soldiers who had laughed at his teetotalism determined to play him a trick. It was a cavalry regi- ment; and they had to ride some distance, taking their rations with them. They took his flask, which he had filled with water, and filled it with brandy. He knew nothing of it, and when they halted for the midday meal, they watched him. Taking his flask, he found it full of brandy; and immediately, while every eye was fixed upon him, he turned the flask upside down, and poured all the brandy on the grass.

A young officer in India found himself serving among very godless comrades, amid the fierce passions which were kindled during the suppression of the Indian mu- tiny. He thought that we were acting mercilessly and unjustly, and he remonstrated. He was severely perse- cuted. " What am I to do ? " he asked of General Outram, the Bayard of India, when he felt deeply de- pressed amid a storm of calumny. " Do you fear God or man ? " asked Outram. " If you fear God, do as you are doing, and bear the insults which are heaped upon you. If you fear man and the mess, let them hang their number of rebels every day." Did not General Gordon's almost magic influence arise from the all-per- vading sense, inspired by his mere presence, that here was a man who always was, and always would be, in- flexibly true to his highest convictions ? When he was in the Soudan he never hesitated to place outside his tent the white handkerchief, which meant, as all men knew, that he was at prayer, and that during the sacred hour when he was alone with God he must not be dis- turbed. The young man who is guided by such prin- ciples, and who has attained to such moral courage, is perfectly certain to succeed in the highest form of possible success, whatever his lot on earth may be.

8. And, after all, the young man in business is situated, as regards companionship, very much like the boy in the public school, or the young man at the universities. His good example will be of priceless value wherever it is exhibited. When Coleridge Patteson was a boy at Eton, he was captain of the eleven; and he had the courage to declare that he would resign his captaincy, and take no part in the rowing, if coarse songs were sung at the annual supper. An objectionable song was sung, and he, with others, at once rose and left the room. It was not until an apology was offered that he resumed his post. When a very great living statesman was at Eton, he used deliberately to turn his glass upside down, before all eyes, if an improper toast was proposed. "When Arthur Cumnock went to Harvard," writes Mr. R. H. Davis, "the fast set had marked him for its own. The manly thing, so the incoming freshmen were told, was to drink and gamble politely, and wire-pull for the societies, and cut recitations. In four years this idea of the manly thing has changed, because the young athlete threw all his influence on the side of temperance in all things, fair play, courtesy, and modesty."

9. But lastly, what a young man will be in business and in life depends upon what he is in his own soul. There can be no perfection of manhood, there can be no nobleness of life, without the grand old eternal virtues of temperance, soberness, and chastity. If a young man cannot say "No" when he is asked to join in sweepstakes, or bet on this or that "event," it may soon be all up with him. There is one jail in England of which

a wing is said to be almost entirely filled with felons who began their downward career by betting and gambling, in a way which they chose to regard as manly and interesting. Tens of thousands in all ranks have been led on the high road to ruin by this detestable epidemic of spurious excitement. He who wishes to be a true man must begin to take the right course as a young man respecting all these matters. He must be sternly on his guard against seductive pleasures. " I have sat upon the shore, and waited for the gradual approach of the sea," wrote Lady M. Wortley Montague, "and have seen the dancing waves and white surf, and admired that He who measured it with His hand had given to it such life and motion ; and I have lingered till its gentle waters grew into billows, and had wellnigh swept me from my firmest footing. So have I seen a heedless youth gazing with a too curious spirit upon the sweet motions and gentle approaches of an inviting pleasure, till it has detained his eye and imprisoned his feet, and swelled upon his soul, and swept him into a swift destruction." If a youth has not character enough, or firmness enough, to resist the Devil amid those serpent-like insinuations or terrible tiger-leaps by which Satan is certain to assault the soul, he may give up all hope of doing well, either in business or in life. He will have nothing to give back to God at last except the dust of a polluted body, and the shipwreck of a lost soul. " So unspeakably poor may a soul go back into the gray mists of nothingness. They may write ' Here lies no one buried,' and then after that let it go as it may." Oh, that every young man, whether in business or not, would bear *this* in mind, — that for the drunkard, the cheat, the liar, the impure, the corrupter of others, there is, short of a deep repentance and a total change, no hope on earth. What is true of the body is true also of the soul. The laws of God are to the moral powers what the laws of nature, so called, are to the physical powers. "Obedience to the laws of nature preserves the bloom and life of the body; obedience to the laws of God preserves the bloom of the soul. 'In all these things is the life of the Spirit.' Moral death, ever enlarging itself, is as inevitable upon a course of sin as speedy mortality upon a course of vice. When sin enters, it brings forth abundantly after its kind; and death is not so much its arbitrary award as its inevitable procreation.'

III.

THE YOUNG MAN IN THE CHURCH.

THE title of this third paper is a little vague. "The Young Man in the Home," and "The Young Man in Business," is equally "The Young Man in the Church." Ninety-nine out of every hundred young men have been baptized into the church of Christ; and even in the few accidental cases where this holy rite has been neglected, they are, in a wider and more eternal sense, members of the church of Christ, because, by the privilege of their human birth, they are members of Christ, the children of God, and inheritors of the kingdom of heaven. Many evils arise from the many different connotations in which the word "church" is used. A little "orientation" on the subject may not be amiss, if it serve to show that by the word "church" we mean nothing clerical or sacerdotal or ecclesiastical or artificial, but simply the universal flock of Christ, of which the Church of England and the various Nonconformist bodies are separate folds. Our Lord only used the word "church" twice in all the discourses recorded in the four Gospels. The word occurs in only two texts of one evangelist (Matt. xvi. 18 ; xviii. 17) ; and in one of those two passages the word is used in the very limited sense of a local body of believers (Matt. xviii. 17) : "If he refuse to hear them, tell it unto the church," where the margin rightly gives "the congregation ; " i.e., of the local synagogue. Only in the words to St. Peter, "On this rock

will I build my church," does Christ use the word in
the common modern sense. His habitual phrase for
"all believers" — to whom, when he had overcome the
sharpness of death, he opened the kingdom of heaven —
was not "the church," but "the kingdom of heaven," or
"the kingdom of God." By "the church," in its general
sense, I never can mean this or that Christian body, and
least of all any Christian body like the Church of Rome,
which, with arrogant anathemas and exorbitant usurpa-
tion, supported for centuries by ambition, forgeries, and
frauds, claims an indefeasible right to regard its special
corruptions as infallible, and to lord it over God's heritage, either with threats and excommunications, or with
the thumbscrew and the stake. I never can mean anything but "all who call upon the name of the Lord
Jesus Christ, both theirs and ours;" all Christians,
wheresoever they may be throughout the world; "the
mystical body of Christ, which is the blessed company
of all faithful people." I am not writing immediately
to the unholy and the unrighteous, the godless and
profane, to liars and perjured persons; I am not
ostensibly addressing those who, having flung the re-
straints of religion, and therewith of all morality, to
the winds, are profane persons, like Esau, who for one
morsel of food sold his birthright; I am not writing
to those who have deliberately plunged into the miserable and meaningless excitement of betters and gamblers,
who have drowned themselves in the deadening brutali-
zation of drink, who are deliberately empoisoning the
fountains of their own being, defiling the flesh, and
speaking evil of dignities. But I *am* speaking to all
young men who have set before them any semblance or
vestige of a high and pure ideal; to all who, what-

ever may be the faults and backslidings which, through
the frailty of our mortal nature, prevent them from
always standing upright, nevertheless desire to be, and
in some measure continue to be, the sheep in Christ's
flock, the scholars in His school, the soldiers in His
army, the honest laborers in His vineyard, the faithful
servants in His house.

Let no reader think that the duties of "the young
man in the church" are lost in the vastness of the
region of work. The sphere of our duties to the church
of God and the brotherhood of man widens round us in
concentric circles, like those which we cause when we
throw a stone into a lake, and the blue rings of ripple
spread round the one point in its broken surface, and do
not cease till they die away upon the shore. Our duties
begin with our own persons, — all that we owe to our
mortal bodies and to our immortal souls. They widen
first to the circle of our immediate home, and of our
entire family ; and thence they spread outwards to our
neighborhood, our parish, our town, our county, our country, our race, the whole race of man. "Every hammer-
stroke on the anvil of duty forges something that shall
outlast eternity." Little duties are great duties because
they are *duties.* In the Arabian legend the Archangel
Gabriel, sent by Allah the Merciful, the Compassionate,
at once to prevent Solomon the Magnificent from falling
into a sin, and to help home a little weary, overbur-
dened yellow ant, which otherwise would have been
drowned in a coming shower, regards either work as
equally dignified, because both alike are done at the
behest of God. Let no young man think that any service which he can render is only small and insignificant,
and therefore that it is hardly worth doing. "First do

the little things well," says the Persian proverb, "and
soon the great things will come begging you to do
them." This is what George Herbert meant to teach
when he wrote : —

> "A servant with this clause
> Makes drudgery divine:
> Who sweeps a room, as for Thy laws,
> Makes that and th' action fine; "

and it was what Robert Browning meant in Pippa's
song : —

> "All service ranks the same with God —
> With God, whose puppets, best or worst,
> Are we — there is no last or first."

This, too, is the meaning of Christ's promise that
even a cup of cold water given in his name to the least
of his little ones shall not lose its reward; and that he
who would be first among us must be last of all, and
servant of all.

1. I have no hesitation in saying that the key-note to
the work of "the young man in the church" will be
struck *by the way in which he uses his Sunday.* If he
regards it as a sacred day, holy to the Lord, honorable,
beloved — if he treats its meditations, its worship, its
communion with God, as a fountain in which he may
constantly wash off "the contagion of the world's slow
stain" — he is utilizing, for his present and eternal good,
one of the simplest yet most precious means of grace.
If he makes it a duty and a rule to draw a distinction
between Sunday and other days; not to forsake the
assembling of ourselves together, as the manner of some
is, but openly to profess himself a Christian by attend-
ing the public worship of Christians; to keep steadily

in mind the lessons which he learnt at his confirmation, or at his admission into church communion; — not to turn his back upon the Supper of the Lord; then these acts of habitual faithfulness will soon be transmuted from self-denials into sources of joy, and, added to his own daily prayers, morning and evening, "at the altar of his own bedside," — will do much, very much, to lead, him in the way everlasting. They will keep his feet now and ever in the paths of wisdom, whose ways are ways of pleasantness, and all her paths are peace. But if, as so many do, he lets the voice of Christian duty as to these things sink first to a faint whisper, and then into indignant silence; if he lets laziness and self-indulgence persuade him to eat the fruit of his own devices; if he pleads that he works hard in the week, and has a right to claim Sunday "for himself;" that sermons are a weariness to the flesh, and services a bore — then the giving up of this open participation in immemorial religious privileges will, times without number, be the first step in a downward career. The young man who neglects the *means* of grace will assuredly not grow in grace. I have seen this again and again. I have read of a young man who, remarking that he "preferred finding sermons in stones to hearing sticks preach," used to be found on Sunday lying under a tree reading "Don Juan." The youth who abandons the requirements of his *religion* too often — and sooner rather than later — begins to sit loose to the inexorable laws of *morality*. A sure indication that a youth is in peril of falling into the clutches of the world, the flesh, and the devil, is when, with slight and contemptible excuses, which do not deceive his better self, he begins to speak his own words, and seek

his own pleasure on the Lord's Day. If godless comrades say to him with a sneer : —

> "What, always dreaming over heavenly things,
> Like angel-heads in stone with pigeon wings?
> Mine be the friend less earnest in his prayers,
> Who takes less interest in his soul's affairs;" —

the only answer is: —

> "Well spoken, advocate of sin and shame,
> Known by thy bleating, Ignorance thy name!"

I am no rigid precisian, no hard, stern, uncompromising
Puritan, in my views of the way in which Sunday
should be hallowed ; I would have it always a glad and
a natural day, as well as a sacred day. But this I say :
Show me two young men, of whom one is regularly seen
in his place in church on Sunday, and tries to make of
the service a real time of prayer and praise; and the
other spends the whole day in reading newspapers, in
riding immense distances on his bicycle, refreshing himself at public-houses by the way, and not interrupting
by one serious word the frivolities of idlest, if not even
of unhallowed, talk, poured forth "in one weak, washy
everlasting flood" — then I know which of the two is
the safer, and which of the two will go to rest at night
the more happy, and at peace with God and with his
own soul.

2. I think that every young man who has any sense
of reverence — of the fear and faith of God, and love to
the Lord Jesus Christ — should definitely identify himself with one church, and with the beneficent work of
that church. It is best if he can attach himself to the
church of his own parish; but if, for any reason, in

that church he finds that, so far as he is concerned, the clergy do not reach him, but —

"When they list their lean and flashy songs
Grate on their scranned pipes of wretched straw —
The hungry sheep look up, and are not fed;" —

then let him, without scruple, join another church. But do not let him be too much in a hurry to judge and reject preachers, or to pass empty, flippant, and conceited criticisms upon them.

"The worst speak something good: if all want sense,
God takes a text, and preacheth patience."

3. But next every young man should regard it as a duty to take some distinct part, however small, in some one definite branch of church activity. He can sing in a choir; or help as a sidesman in seating the congregation and collecting the offertory; or take a class in the Sunday-school; or go out with the lads to their cricket or football on Saturdays; or manage a penny bank; or be secretary of an institute; or teach all the lads in the school to swim; or be officer in a boys' brigade; or help to organize pleasant evenings for the people; or share in the training of a gymnasium; or undertake secretarial work; or visit in a slum; or twenty other things, which will help to identify him with the beneficent service of others, and deepen in his mind the conviction that the service of the poor, the young, and the ignorant is much too sacred a thing to be delegated to the clergy only. We cannot do by proxy our duty to our neighbor. It is the common work of the whole church of God; and young men, as members of the church, have their share in the general responsibility. And these two things I can tell them, — one, that they will soon find, in

any real and self-denying work thus undertaken, not a
disagreeable burden, but a source of personal advantage,
and much happy experience; the other, that this form of
altruism, whatever it may be, must not be regarded as a
mere insignificant adjunct of life, but as the one thing
which gives to a young man's life its best dignity and
its most essential importance. I have known not a few
youths who have owed their entire position and rise in
life to that faithfulness which led them to take part
in the work of the church of God.

4. Let us, as in the former cases, look at one or two
contrasts.

I. Here is the career of one of the world's millions
of prodigals, ending, as all such careers must do, in
collapse, and, unless repentance comes in time, in final
catastrophe. It is one of the most marvellous of the
mysteries of iniquity that, in the lives of crowds of
young men, all the accumulated experience of the past
history of the world goes for so very little. This is the
lesson taught in that "unwritten saying" attributed to
Christ by Mohammedan tradition : —

"Jesus once said, 'The world is like a deceitful
woman, who, when asked how many husbands she had
had, answered, "so many that she could not count them.
I murdered and got rid of them." It is strange,' said
Jesus, 'that the rest had so little wisdom that, in spite
of your cruel treatment of others, they took no warning,
and still burned with love for you.' "

The youth of whom I speak — his name was well
known, and he is dead, but I will not mention it, for
I allude to him not to condemn *him*, but to warn others
— was one of high genius and brilliant promise. He
was the only son of a clergyman; gifted far beyond

most youths with a handsome person and a fine intel-
lect. While yet young he fell — no matter how, no
matter where — into the snares of the sorceress, with
the result which no transgressor can ever escape. Even
the Greeks knew that he who listened to the song of the
Sirens will be dashed in hopeless shipwreck upon the
bone-strewn isles ; that the magic cup of Circe — her
"orient liquor in a crystal glass" — was a cup which

> "The visage quite transforms of him who drinks,
> And the inglorious likeness of a beast
> Fixes instead, unmoulding reason's mintage
> Charactered in the face."

One who knew best this youth of whom I speak, and
tried to love him even in his degradation, was forced
thus to allude to him : —

"I once had the opportunity of contemplating near at hand
an example of the results produced by a course of interesting
and romantic domestic treachery. No golden halo of fiction
was about this example. I saw it bare and real, and it was very
loathsome. I saw a mind degraded by the practice of mean sub-
terfuge, by the habit of perfidious deception, and a body depraved by the infectious influence of the vice-polluted soul. I
had suffered much from the forced and prolonged view of this
spectacle : those sufferings I did not now regret, for their simple
recollection acted as a most wholesome antidote to temptation.
*They had inscribed on my reason the conviction that unlawful
pleasure . . . is delusive and envenomed pleasure — its hollow-
ness disappoints at the time, its poison cruelly tortures afterwards, its effects deprave forever.*"

This youth died, — died prematurely, died miserably;
and his sister wrote : —

"We have buried our dead out of sight. . . . It is not per-
mitted us to grieve for him who is gone, as others grieve for
those whom they love. The removal of our only brother must

be regarded rather in the light of a mercy than a chastisement. He was his father's and his sisters' pride in boyhood, . . . but it has been our lot to see him take a wrong bent; to hope, expect, await his return to the right path; to know the sickness of hope deferred, the dismay of prayer baffled; to experience despair at last; and now to behold the sudden, early, obscure close of what might have been a noble career — the wreck of talent, the ruin of promise, the untimely, dreary extinction of what might have been a burning and shining light. Nothing remains of him but a memory of errors and sufferings. There is such a bitterness of pity for his life and death, such a yearning for the emptiness of his whole existence, as I cannot describe. I seemed to receive an impressive revelation of the feebleness of humanity; of the inadequacy of even genius to lead to true greatness unaided by religion and principle."

ii. With such a life — so deplorably wasted on the bitter longing for, and the yet bitterer fruition of, the passions of dishonor — the life, alas ! of many thousands, and usually begun in boyhood or youth — compare the work which young men of a nobler stamp and of purer hearts have achieved in the church of God.

A young man had gained a prize for a Latin essay at Cambridge in 1784. The subject of the essay was " Is Involuntary Servitude Justifiable ? " He recited the essay in June, and then mounted his horse to ride to his home in London. On his way he thought over the shocking facts of the slave-trade, and grew so much agitated that he dismounted, and, sitting down to think, came to the conclusion, " If this be so, slavery must be put down." He determined to devote himself to the cause of freeing England from the disgrace of " using the arm of freedom to rivet the fetters of the slave." For twenty-two years he labored amid many difficulties and dangers. Twenty-two years afterwards, and in no small measure through him, the slave-trade was abol-

ished in 1807 by Act of Parliament. Twenty-six years
after that, in 1833, the existing slaves were emanci-
pated. An obelisk now stands on the spot which wit-
nessed the self-consecration of his life. The name of
that youth was Thomas Clarkson, and the result of
his work in the church was the protection and happiness of hundreds of thousands of the most oppressed
and miserable of mankind.

A little more than a century ago there was a poor
young Baptist cobbler at Kettering in Northampton-
shire. He was by no means a good cobbler; and a gentleman who wanted to employ him sometimes gave him
two pairs of boots to make, on the off chance of getting
a right and left which should be reasonably wearable.
He eked out his very slender earnings by teaching in
the village school. This youth was oppressed by the
thought that while Christianity was only represented by
a few twinkling points of light in vast regions of the
globe, there were areas of thousands of square miles
over which darkness covered the lands, and gross darkness the peoples. He used to weep as he showed to his
poor village scholars a map of which so vast an extent
represented only the blackness of heathendom. He
became a minister in the little Baptist community, and
urged on his brethren the burning conviction of our
duty to the heathen world which pervaded his own soul.
"Young man," said the senior minister, "sit down. If
God wants to convert the world, He will do so without
your help." But the youth persevered. He preached
on "Enlarge the stakes of thy tent;" and the offertory
amounted to £13 2s. 6d. The world laughed consu-
medly through all its organs and societies at the thirteen
pounds two and sixpence, and the host of "consecrated

cobblers" who were to convert the heathen millions.
But that youth was named WILLIAM CAREY; and ere he
died he had translated the Bible into some of the chief
vernacular Bibles of India, and given the first mighty
impulse to those missions which, from the Himalayas to
Cape Comorin, have undermined the monstrous idola-
tries of Hindostan.

Take but one instance more. Some seventy years
ago a Harrow boy of noble birth was standing not far
from the school gates, when he saw with indignation
the horrible levity with which some drunken men were
conducting a pauper funeral: —

> "Rattle his bones over the stones,
> He's only a pauper, whom nobody owns!"

Then and there that generous boy dedicated himself to
defend through life the cause of the oppressed, to pity
the sorrowful sighing of the prisoners, and to see that
those in need and necessity had their rights. To this
high service he felt himself to be anointed as by the
hands of invisible consecration, and nobly was his vow
fulfilled. He saved the little chimneysweeps from the
brutalities to which they were subjected. He mitigated
or cancelled the horrors of factories and mines. He
founded ragged schools. He helped the poor coster-
mongers. He went about like the knights of old redress-
ing human wrongs. To few men has it been given to
achieve more for the amelioration of the human race.
He passed, as all the best and bravest men pass, through
hurricanes of calumny, and felt the heartsickness of
hope deferred amid painful isolation. Never was there
a more remarkable and beautiful sight than that of his
funeral in Westminster Abbey. "For departed kings

there are appointed honors, and the wealthy have their gorgeous obsequies. It was his nobler lot to clothe a nation in spontaneous mourning, and to sink into the grave amid the benedictions of the poor." His name was ANTONY ASHLEY, EARL OF SHAFTESBURY. His statue stands by the western gate of the great Abbey in marble not whiter than his life; and the two mighty monosyllables carved upon it : —

LOVE   SERVE

are the best epitome of the best work of " the young man in the church."

IV.

THE YOUNG MAN AND MARRIAGE.

THE world in general laughed heartily at Mr. Punch's "Advice to those who are about to marry," which, on turning the page, was found to consist of the one word, "DON'T." As a universal rule the advice would be very bad advice. The causes which led to the neglect and avoidance of marriage in the decadence alike of Greece and Rome were the vilest and most degrading causes possible. They were deeply seated vice and degrading selfishness. In Greece they culminated rapidly in the collapse of all nobleness and power — "the fading of all glory into darkness, and of all strength into dust." The Greek — the hero of Marathon and Salamis, the patriot of Thermopylæ, who deemed it sufficient epitaph. —

> "Go tell the Spartans, thou who passest by,
> That here, obedient to their laws, we lie," —

soon dwindled by luxury and sensualism into the *Græculus esuriens* of whom Juvenal drew so contemptuous and indignant a picture. The Roman, whose iron arms and dauntless courage had subdued the world, sank into the corrupt and effeminate dandy who cared only for his own degraded comfort, until Rome "saw her glories star by star expire," and she : —

> " . . . whom mightiest kingdoms curtsied to,
> Like a forlorn and desperate castaway,
> Did shameful execution on herself."

Even in the days of Augustus, and increasingly under the later emperors, the state felt it necessary to interfere with vicious self-indulgence, in the instinct of national self-preservation. Laws were passed conferring distinctions and privileges on those who had three children born in honorable wedlock; and a selfish celibacy was branded with reprobation. Long before those days, in the dramas of Plautus and Terence, the conclusion always turns on the young man's marriage; and the fathers never feel themselves secure until that event has been happily arranged. The encouragement of marriage, and its felt sacredness, have been the chief element in the vitality of the Jews; and the books, both sacred and secular, of that most religious of the ancient nations, abound in eulogies upon the blessedness of marriage, until in the days of the Talmudists it became a fixed disgrace for a Jew not to have married by the age of twenty-one.

"A Jew who has no wife," says the Talmud, "is not a man; for it is said, 'Male and female created He them.'" And again: "From the age of twenty, if a man lives in celibacy, he lives in constant transgression. Up to that age, the Holy One (blessed be He!) waits for him to enter into the state of matrimony, and curses his bones if he does not marry then." I do not suppose that Lord Tennyson had ever read this passage from the "Mishñah," yet he says much the same: —

> "'Alone,' I said, 'from earlier than I know,
> Immersed in rich foreshadowings of the world,
> I loved the woman: he that doth not, lives
> A drowning life, besotted in sweet self,
> Or pines in sad experience worse than death,
> Or keeps his winged affections clipt with crime.'"

It is not, however, my object to dwell on the many

dangers and disadvantages of a purely selfish or vicious celibacy. I am addressing those who mean, God willing, to enter on the married state, and who, even now, find in a true and pure love an antidote against temptation, and a bond of moral faithfulness to their future wives — a bond founded not only upon chivalry, but upon the loftiest religious motives.

I. Are there, then, *none* who are about to marry, who, nevertheless, would do well to bear in mind the imperious monosyllabic dissuasion *Don't?* Yes, there are some, and it is important that on *them* this advice should be impressed.

1. If, for instance, a young man knows that he has *incapacitated* himself by the retributive consequences of past transgressions from a pure and healthy marriage, then, if he have indeed repented of unlawful deeds, he is bound to remember that he has forfeited the right to a hallowed union, and that it would be, on his part, a consummate baseness to entail on an innocent wife, and on innocent children yet unborn, the fearful Nemesis which is to him the brand of God upon forbidden indulgences. If, again, though he have himself been perfectly innocent, he knows that in his family there is the confirmed and hereditary taint of scrofula, of malformation, of idiocy, or of consumption, then he should feel that, by the voice of inevitable circumstances, God calls to him for a great self-renunciation. Let him not moan that the call is too hard upon him. God never withholds his immense compensations from those who, for his sake, give up father or mother, or wife or children. In proportion to the greatness of the self-sacrifice shall they receive the hundredfold reward. I knew one who had thus voluntarily given up. He was

a saint of God; and if ever there was a man to whose
sad heart the sweet companionship of a loving woman
would have brought a boundless consolation for life's
many troubles, it was he.   But his father and his uncle
had died by their own hands, and there had been other
warning calamities in his family.   He feared that the
taint of madness might, in due time, reveal itself in
him also; though, for long years of manhood, nothing
could have been more holy and useful than his life, and
more sound than his intelligence.   So he made his resolve that he would never marry; that it was better for
society that his race should end with him.   His surmise
proved true.   Had he married, the end might have been
some terrible tragedy.   He died, peaceful and happy, in
an asylum which sheltered and secured him from the
development of homicidal mania.

2. There is another hindrance to the lawfulness of
marriage which ought never to be overlooked: it is
hopeless poverty, or entire uncertainty of any continuous means of earning a livelihood.   To marry like brute
beasts which have no understanding, as is sometimes
done by mere boys and girls in the slums, within half a
crown of destitution, or with no more secure promise
of maintenance than a chance job of a week or two,
is mere revolting selfishness and animal degradation.
These are the marriages which blight society with the
prolific birth of a feeble, stunted, half-starved, vicious,
and semi-idiotic offspring, to be the curse of a future
generation.   If a man has no sufficient means to maintain a wife and family, his marriage does but kick
against the ordinance of his destiny.   His selfishness
will not only inevitably doom himself to grinding care
and crushing anxiety, but he will drag down his wife

and children into the pitiless abyss of hunger and misery. Be he clergyman or layman, the man who has no sufficient means on which to marry commits a crime against society if he marries on the chance of something "turning up." To such persons nothing ever does "turn up." They are like the old lady who felt sure that it was going to rain, but said "that she would trust to Providence to send her an umbrella."

3. But if in a man's own person or circumstances there be no such divinely appointed hindrance, he is none the less bound to be careful in his choice of the partner of his life. The young man who chooses his bride from a family in which there is much consumption, or other fatal heredity, prepares for himself hereafter the misery of bereavement and the certainty of many blighted hopes. If a young man have any calmness of judgment, he will consider the extreme desirability that the mother of his children should be one whose health and strength and intelligence will leave them the lifelong legacy of a sound mind in a sound body. And here let no one say that these are cold-blooded calculations, which are swept away as with a flood by "falling in love." To fall in love wildly, inconsiderately, imprudently, hastily, with no control of sense, reason, or conscience, is to follow a blind and impetuous instinct, and to behave otherwise than duty requires in the most solemn event of life. The marriage of the maid who was engaged to a stranger when she went into the garden to cut a cabbage is scarcely likely to be a happy one. A young man may be suddenly taken by a pretty face; but if that be the sole qualification in his future wife, he may find too soon that "favor is deceitful, and beauty vain; but a prudent wife is from the Lord."

4. I should advise a young man to think twice before he marries an untidy girl. I have been a guest in houses where everything was revolting from this cause, and where one scarcely ventured to open a drawer in the guest-chamber for fear of what one might find in it. Certainly, in respect to a man's home, "cleanliness is next to godliness," and untidiness means squalor and waste. Few old friends will care to visit a man who has a slatternly wife, and children whose faces in consequence are not kept sweet and clean. A young lady once asked her lover to direct a letter for her. He did it so hastily that the direction was blotted and illegible. She blushed as he handed it back to her, and from that moment her affection for him began visibly to cool. The engagement never came off; and as he recounted the circumstance, he was magnanimous enough to observe that "she had been more than half right."

5. And most assuredly the young man who finally chooses his bride without having good reason to be sure that her *temper* is as a rule sweet and equable, is taking a rash step, and one which he may rue through many a bitter year.

> " Look you! the gray mare
> Is ill to live with, when her whinny shrills
> From tile to scullery, and her small goodman
> Shrinks in his arm-chair, while the fires of hell
> Mix with his hearth."

This, at least, is the recorded experience of three thousand years. "It is better," says the wise king, "to dwell in the corner of the housetop, than with a brawling woman in a wide house;" and "the contentions of a wife are a continuous dropping." Petruccio was profoundly wise in taming his Shrew before he became her victim. Nor is there any real necessity for making a wrong choice by mistake. A young man is supremely foolish if he marries a girl about whom he knows little or nothing. The face may be some index, but it may unconsciously lead to very mistaken conclusions. If, however, a young man has made many opportunities of being in the society of his intended bride before he takes the irrevocable step of binding himself to her in a bond which cannot be dissolved, then he must be more than usually obtuse if, by her bearing to her father and mother, to her brothers and sisters, to her companions, to the old and to the young, he is not very well able to gauge her character. And if he sees that, though she may show herself in the best light to *him* individually, she reveals a strong undercurrent of selfishness in her character, I should advise him to pause in time. I once knew an eminent person, who was in character a man of singular geniality and buoyancy of spirits, but who, for what reason I never could make out, married a hard, harsh, angular, unattractive wife. What the lady may have been to him I do not know; but certain it is that whereas before his marriage he had been surrounded by troops of friends, yet after his marriage hardly one of them, much as they continued to love and honor him, ever entered his house. His wife, whether from parsimony, or religion gone sour, or inherent " cussedness," turned the cold shoulder on them; and if they called once they were never encouraged to call again. A wife without sympathy may cost a man the loss of all his friends.

6. If there be one *Phylloxera vastatrix* of wedded happiness more fatal in its ravages than another; if there be one intruder into this vineyard which, more surely than any other, will cause its root to be as rot-

tenness, and its blossom to go up as dust, — it is *intemper-
ance*. I recall many a harrowing example of this curse
and corruption — this heavy blow and sad discourage-
ment — in wedded lives, which it has been my fate to
witness. No more certain, no more absolute, collapse of
happiness can be even conceived. I remember one, about
whose wife persons soon began to ask how her strange
demeanor could be accounted for; why she was so often
heavy and stupid and odd in her behavior; why at
others she showed a sort of spurious hilarity? And
the answer could not be long in coming: she was by
position a lady, but she drank. I recall the young man,
exceptionally prosperous in his position, with all life
stretching before him in apparent brightness, married to
the shallow, showy, arrogant, domineering woman, with
her dress and her extravagance and her fashionableness
of sham religion, — who, unable to control this domestic scourge, took to drinking his bottle of port wine
every day at dinner. He sank lower and lower into
debt, lost his clients, failed to pay the bills of his wine-
merchant, went all downhill into shabbiness and disgrace, and so ruined himself, and bequeathed ruin to his
children after him. I recall the man, respectable and
diligent, who came to me weeping, to say that, at all
costs, he must leave his home; at all costs he must turn
his back on his country; at all costs he must separate
from his wife, for she was slowly dragging him down
into the abyss, and had again and again brought him
into misery and confusion by selling for drink every
stick of his furniture, and causing such scenes of violence and shame that, if they continued, he knew not
what tragedy might come of them. I recall another —
a fine, stalwart man — who came to ask my advice what

he should do, since his wife, in his necessary absence at work, pawned for drink the very clothes and boots of his boys, so that it was impossible for them to go to school. To every young man, of the poorer and lower middle classes especially, I should say, " If you are a total abstainer, and if your future wife is a total abstainer, from intoxicating drink, there is, at any rate, *one* sunken reef which has caused many a horrible shipwreck, from the peril of which the ship of your life will be kept free.

II. I have spoken of the choice of a bride, let me now speak of marriage itself.

1. Even if the young man and his bride are free from egregious faults and dangerous tendencies, marriage may still become a failure and a misery if it leads to an autocratic tyranny either of wife or of husband ; or to the worse alternative of an incessant clash and conflict of opposing wills. " You must take two *bears* with you into your home, my dear," said a quaint old lady to her nephew, " if you want to be happy." — " Two *bears ?* " he asked in astonishment. " Yes," she said, " bear and forbear." It was extremely wise advice. In marriage, where it is the true union of hearts, there still must be give and take ; and each must be glad, many a time, to prefer what in the abstract he would like less, because it is the cherished wish of one dearer to him than himself. How well Milton puts it in the lines : —

"She as a veil down to the slender waist
Her unadornèd golden tresses wore
Dishevelled, but in wanton ringlets waved,
As the vine waves her tendrils; which implied
Subjection, but required with gentle sway,
And by her yielded, by him best received,
Yielded with coy submission, honest pride,
And sweet, reluctant, amorous delay."

Yes! but the fundamental "*subjection*" must often be suffered to become a happy dominance by the voluntary tenderness which seeketh not its own, and is not easily provoked.

2. Where there is found in well-assorted marriages this lowly wisdom of the self-sacrifice which love transmutes into delight, there marriage, which Christ himself "adorned and beautified with his presence, and first miracle which he wrought in Cana of Galilee," becomes indeed a flower rescued from the Lost Paradise. It has been so in all ages; for it is an ordinance of God himself, from the beginning, that "they twain shall be one flesh." We know the pictures of Holy Writ. In the Old Testament we read of the happy homes of Abraham, of Isaac, of Boaz, of Jesse with his group of splendid sons. "Whoso findeth a wife, findeth a good thing," says Solomon. "Live joyfully," says the Preacher, " with the wife whom thou lovest all the days of thy vanity." " A good wife is a good portion," says the son of Sirac: "she shall be given into the bosom of them that fear the Lord." In the New Testament, perhaps a thousand years later, we read that, "marriage is honorable in all, and a bed undefiled."

3. Here, again, is the beautiful picture drawn by a Christian writer, Tertullian, in the third century. "How happy," he says, "is the marriage which Heaven approves! How shall I suffice to describe the felicity of that marriage which the church unites, and the sacrament confirms, and the blessing seals; which angels make known, and the Father holds for valid! How blest the wedding of two of the faithful of one hope, one discipline, one service! Both are brethren, both fellow-servants. Together they pray; together they

instruct, exhort, and uphold one another. They are
alike in the church of God, in the feasts of God, in
straits, in persecutions, in consolations. Neither avoids
the other ; neither is stern to the other. Freely they
visit the sick, they help the poor. Christ, seeing and
hearing such things, rejoices. To them he sends his
peace. Where the two are there is he, and there the
Evil One is not." Truly such a marriage is "the queen
of friendships " and "the nursery of heaven."

And to show that this is no mere ideal picture of the
past, here is the testimony of a modern novelist, which
I quote because it is full of beauty and wise sugges-
tiveness : —

"He a gentleman; she a wifely wife, a motherly
mother, and a lady. This, then, is a happy couple.
Their life is full of purpose and industry, yet lightened
by gayety. There the divine institution, marriage, takes
its natural colors ; and it is at once pleasant and good to
catch such glimpses of Heaven's designs, and sad to
think how often the great boon accorded by God to man
and woman must have been abused ere it could have
sunk to be the standing joke and butt of farce writers
and the theme of weekly punsters.

"In this pair we see the wonders a male and a female
may do for each other in the sweet bond of holy wedlock. In that blessed relation alone two interests are
really one, and two hearts lie safe at anchor side by
side.

"They are friends — for they are man and wife.

"They are lovers still — for they are man and wife.

"They are one forever — for they are man and wife.

"This wife brightens the house from kitchen to garret
for her husband ; this husband works like a king for

his wife. They share all troubles, and by sharing halve them. They share all pleasures, and by sharing double them. They climb the hill together now; and when, by the inevitable law they begin to descend towards the dark valley, they will still go hand in hand, smiling so tenderly, and supporting each other with a care more lovely than when the arm was strong and the foot firm. What terrors has old age for this happy pair? It cannot make them ugly; for though the purple light of youth recedes, a new kind of tranquil beauty — the aloe blossom of many years of innocence — comes to, and sits like a dove upon the aged faces, where goodness, sympathy, and intelligence have harbored together and long, and where evil passions have flitted (for we are all human), but found no resting-place." [1]

Such is a marriage begun in the high spirit of the prince who says to his bride : —

> " My wife, my life ! O we will walk this world,
> Yoked in all exercise of noble end,
> And so through those dark gates across the wild
> That no man knows."

Certainly, then, we advise a young man to marry so it be a wise marriage, so it be a prudent marriage. Only let him enter upon this crisis of his life not " unadvisedly, lightly, and wantonly," but " discreetly, advisedly, soberly, and in the fear of God, duly considering the causes for which matrimony was ordained." It was ordained both for the foundation of happy homes, and the continuance of the life of men to other generations; and also " for the society, help, and comfort that one ought to have of the other both in prosperity and adversity."

[1] C. Reade, "Christie Johnstone."

Then will marriage become the best of moral safeguards; the most urgent of generous inspirations, to work and effort; the most precious solace amid the burdens, cares, and anxieties of life.

"My wife, my child," so sings the Chartist poet, Ernest Jones: —

> "My wife, my child, come close to me;
> The world we know is a stormy sea;
> With your hands in mine, if your eyes but shine,
> I care not how wild the storms may be.
>
> For the fiercest wind that ever blew
> Is nothing to me if I shelter you;
> No warmth do I lack, for the howl at my back
> Sings down to my heart, 'Man bold and true!'
>
> A pleasant sail, my child, my wife,
> O'er a pleasant sea to many is life:
> The wind blows warm, and they fear no storm,
> And wherever they go kind friends are rife.
>
> But, wife and child, the love, the love
> That lifteth us to the saints above,
> Could only have grown where storms have blown,
> The truth and strength of the heart to prove."

Immensely different from the stormy life of Ernest Jones was the sunshine of fashionable society amid which Tom Moore lived; but if the former found the peace at home which was not possible to him in the midst of impassioned controversies, the latter, when he too experienced that applause and popularity may turn to ashes, and that all which the world can give is thrice-doubled emptiness, found in *his* home also something better than the world could either give or take away. In the touching lines on his birthday, — the best and truest that he ever wrote, — when he confesses that if

he had it in his power to obliterate the past, but little of
it should stay, he adds that all should be erased : —

> "All but that freedom of the mind
>   Which has been more than wealth to me;
> Those friendships, in my boyhood twined,
>   And kept till now unchangingly;
> And one dear home — one saving ark,
>   Where love's true light at last I've found,
> Shining within, when all was dark,
>   And comfortless, and stormy round."

To every young man, therefore, I would say again,
that, if God gives him the grace of a pure and happy
marriage, he gives him a very rose of Paradise.   And
when he has reverently plucked it, he will soon learn
to say : —

> "Hail, wedded love! mysterious law — true source
> Of human offspring, sole propriety
> In Paradise, of all things common else.
> By thee adulterous lust was driven from men,
> Among the bestial herds to range; by thee
> Founded in reason, loyal, just, and pure
> Relations dear, and all the charities
> Of father, son, and brother first were known.
>
>   .   .   .   .
>
> Here Love his golden shafts employs; here lights
> His constant lamp, and waves his purple wings;
> Reigns here and revels.

V.

THE YOUNG MAN MASTER OF HIMSELF.

FEELING the warmest and kindest interest in the welfare of young men, I have written on "The Young Man in the Home," "The Young Man in Business," "The Young Man in Married Life," and "The Young Man in the Church;" but one more paper is imperatively needed if the others are to have their due influence. It is, in fact, the necessary *prelude* to the others. It is on "The Young Man Master of Himself." Unless he be *this*, the young man will not fulfil his highest ideal in any other sphere. His life, even if it be externally prosperous, cannot but be a failure; yes, and the worst of failures. For the worst of failures for any human being is not to be poor, or insignificant, or outwardly unfortunate, but to be the slave of his lower nature. Many of the best and noblest of the human race — the prophets and the saints of God — have been hated, persecuted, outcast; they have wandered about in sheepskins and goatskins, in dens and caves of the earth, being destitute, afflicted, tormented; and many of them have been tortured not accepting deliverance. Nor has this been the case only with the heroes of faith. Not a few of the rarest human souls have had to bear all through life "the slings and arrows of outrageous fortune." Of our great poet Spenser, his admirer, Phineas Fletcher, wrote in his "Purple Island:" —

> "Yet all his hopes were crossed, his suits deny'd;
> Discouraged, scorned, his writings vilified,
> Poorly, poor man, he lived; poorly, poor man, he died;"

and we know how often the starry soul of Milton found itself —

> "Fallen on evil days and evil tongues,
> In darkness, and with dangers compassed round,
> And solitude."

What hope was there that a noble heart could find itself at ease amid the barbarous dissonance of Bacchus and his revellers, in the bad days of the Stuart Restoration? A man must have made very small progress in the true estimate of life if he has not learnt that what most men regard as failure may be the most splendid success, and what they regard as enviable success may be the most abject of failures. Every young man should lay it down as an axiom that: —

> "Self-reverence, self-knowledge, self-control,
> These three *alone* lead life to sovereign power."

In the window of a room in Queen's College, Oxford, there is an inscription which records that it was once occupied by our young hero-king, Henry V., who is finely described as —

> " VICTOR HOSTIUM ET SUI,"

conqueror not only of his enemies, but of himself. He conquered his enemies at Azincour; but the conquest of himself — the turning of the rout caused by his earlier follies into resistance, and of the resistance into victory — required a far more earnest struggle. How many of the world's laurelled victors have driven their foes

before them on many a battlefield, and yet have hopelessly succumbed to the domestic foes in their own
heart! They have been defeated by their own lower
self : —

> "This coward with pathetic voice,
> Who craves for rest and ease, and joys,
> Myself arch-traitor to myself,
> My hollowest friend, my deadliest foe,
> My clog whatever road I go."

Alexander won the day at Issus, the Granicus, and Ar-
bela, and founded one of the most colossal and enduring
of the empires of the world, before he was thirty-three
years old ; yet, hopelessly subdued by his own baser instincts, the glorious young Greek died as a fool dieth,
drunken and debauched, at Babylon. Napoleon I. won
a hundred terrible battles amid all the pomp and circumstance of magnificent war ; yet, when he was flung
to die on a barren Atlantic rock, he was so utterly de-
void of the most ordinary magnanimity, that he con-
descended to incessant and ignoble squabbles with Sir
Hudson Lowe about etiquette and champagne. On the
other hand, there have been many men whose *outward*
foes have triumphed over them; on whom death has
fallen before they were able to see one of their high
ends accomplished; who have stood pilloried, *because* of
their goodness, " on Infamy's high stage ; " who have
ended their sad careers amid clouds and thick darkness,
in the dungeon, on the scaffold, or at the stake, — who
have yet earned the most immortal palms, and for
whom " all the trumpets have sounded on the other
side." Is not the life of Christ the eternal type of such
glorious failures ? And have not the " masters of those
who know " expressed their adhesion to the supremacy

of this ideal? Who has not heard the universal Christian proverbs, "*Via crucis, via lucis*," and " No cross, no crown " ? Does not Dante sing : —

> " For not on flowery beds, nor under shade
> Of canopy reposing, Heaven is won " ?

But let no young man suppose that the Ideal of the Cross is an ideal of abjectness or misery. It is, on the contrary, an ideal of glorious supremacy and of a permanent blessedness — yes, even of an exultation — which the world can neither give nor take away. The worst apparent sufferers in the cause of righteousness have felt, in the depths of their anguish, a joy surpassing the joy of harvest. They have been " *contenti nel fuoco* " — " content even in the fire." [1] There has often been a radiancy on the faces of martyrs, as they uplifted their trembling hands out of the flames, such as has never gleamed beneath the diadems or coronals of earthly bliss. And, on the other hand, men who have risen from peasants to emperors have re-echoed with one voice the Wise King's epitaph of thrice-doubled emptiness upon the most consummate splendors of the world. They have exclaimed with Tiberius that " all the gods and goddesses were continually destroying him ;" and with Septimius Severus, "*Omnia fui et nihil expedit,*" — " I have been everything, and it is all of no avail." And why is this? It is because the only real, the only eternal secret of anything which can remotely be called happiness, depends in no respect on external things. The sources of joy and glory lie solely within us. If a man's heart be not at peace; if he does not

---

[1] Dante, "Inferno," l. 118.

possess his own approval ; if a peaceful conscience does
not shed its light upon him — then *nothing* can make
him happy.   For then he has been, in some way or
other, practically false to his own best impulses and
purest aspirations, and : —

> " The worst of miseries
> Is when a nature, framed for noblest things,
> Condemns itself in youth to petty joys,
> And, sore ·athirst for air, breathes scanty life,
> Gasping from out the shallows."

We learn these truths, as we learn all other truths, best
from Scripture.   Our Lord taught us that " a man's life
consisteth not in the abundance of things that he pos-
sesseth " (Luke xii. 15) ; and St. Paul describes Christians as " having nothing, and yet possessing all things."

The secret, then, of all happiness, of all nobleness, of
all true success, is self-mastery, self-possession.

It might well seem strange that our *self* — the inmost
secret of our being — all that constitutes our true immortality, is not *given* us with ourselves, but has to be
acquired by us.   We have, so to speak, to *earn* the
essential reality of our own being.

Ordinary language shows how little this conception
is realized.   By " self-possession," in common speech,
is merely meant that a man does not exhibit outward
signs of emotion or alarm at any sudden crisis ; that he
is master of all facial expression ; that he can conceal
the agitation or excitement which is shown by others.
And when society speaks of a youth as being " *his own
master*," it only means to say that he has a private in-
come of his own, and can do what he likes !

But the true conceptions of " self-possession " and
" being our own masters," so far from these lying on

the surface, are connected with the very depths of our human nature.

Our nature is not simple, but complex; and its perfectness and blessedness consist in the harmonious interrelation of its tendencies and forces. We have acquired ourselves when we have learnt to give the supremacy to what is *best* and *most eternal* within ourselves, and to keep in resolute control all base and destructive elements within us.

This truth forced itself even upon the Pagan moralists, and was seen with marvellous insight especially by Plato.[1] He described man as a tripartite being, consisting of the combination of a lion, a many-headed monster, and a man. The lion represents the passions of the soul, not necessarily ignoble, but liable to become ungovernable, and then destructive. The monster — "a multitudinous polycephalous beast, having a ring of heads of all manner of beasts, tame and wild " — represents the lusts of the flesh. The man represents the reason. Nothing, says Socrates, is more fatal than "to feast the multitudinous monster, and strengthen the lion, but to starve and weaken the man." The human being has only achieved his true destiny when the man is absolute sovereign over the lion, controlling all its impulses; and when he has crushed the many-headed monster beneath his feet. But it is only the few who do not allow the lion and the monster to overthrow and tyrannize over the reason, — and then the man becomes earthly, animal, demonish.

Practically, then, every man is living in one of three conditions, (1) that of defeat; (2) that of uncertain struggle; or (3) that of secure victory.

[1] Plato, "Republic," ix. p. 588.

1. The condition of absolute human defeat presents the spectacle which combines in itself all the most terrible mysteries and all the most consummate tragedies of our earthly life. It has many degrees; it may not always imply a total and hopeless abjectness; but it exists whenever a man has allowed himself to become the slave of his lowest, and especially of his animal impulses. Well may Shakespeare exclaim : —

> "Give me that man
> That is not passion's slave, and I will wear him
> In my heart's core, yea, in my heart of hearts." [1]

Many a man is nothing more nor less than "passion's slave," and there is no servitude more grinding or more disastrous. The duty imposed upon us by nature, by reason, by conscience, by Scripture, by every voice of God without us and within, bids us fight against our evil passions, and make them "come to heel by a strong will, the servant of a tender conscience." The man who tampers with, who makes concessions to, his lower instincts, is lost. For we are, as Aristotle said, naturally "propense to over-indulgence rather than to moderation." [2] The only way to master ourselves is to resist the beginnings of evil; to resist the evil inclination at its very source; to crush the unborn serpent in its gleaming shell. If we dabble with it, if we parley with it, if we pamper the devil within us, nothing but a miracle of grace can save us. We cannot make harmless "covenants with death," or safe "agreements with hell." For instance, the experience of the world shows the enormous strength of sensual impulses; yet no human

---

[1] Shakespeare, "Hamlet," iii. 2.

[2] Εὐκατάφοροί ἐσμεν πρὸς ἀκολασίαν μᾶλλον ἢ πρὸς κοσμιότητα, Aristotle, "Eth. N." ii. 8. 8.

being was ever born who could not have lived, as hundreds of thousands have lived, lives pure and temperate. But the *condition* of doing so is resistance; it is to harden ourselves against ourselves; it is to avail ourselves of the divine grace which is freely and always within the reach of all who seek it. If a man thinks that he can plunge into the rushing and whirling stream and not be swept away by it; that he can walk in the dark along the edge of the precipice and run no risk of shattering fall; that any flowery band will be strong enough in which to check his full-fed appetites when they crash out upon him, "terrible and with a tiger's leaps," he will find, by fatal experience renewed to the human race since the day of —

"That crude apple which perverted Eve,"

that to encourage temptation is to abandon the true mastery of self. How can *he* escape impurity who listens to, and is ever recalling to his self-polluted imagination, the Siren's song? who thinks that he may safely defile the inner sanctities of his moral being, and yet not do so by outward act? who by impure literature, and every other form of unhallowed stimulus, feeds and strengthens the very passions which can only be tamed into temperance, soberness, and chastity by rigid avoidance or determined battle?

Or take the awful desecration of drunkenness. Can there be a more abjectly pitiable spectacle, can there be a more fearfully dismantled hulk on the rolling waters, or a more ghastly wreck upon life's lonely shore, than the habitual drunkard? He cannot resist a chemical product; he has made himself the negro-slave of a dead thing; he has impawned that which is divine within

him to the meanest and loathliest of all the fiends.
"If the glass of brandy were there," — such a miserable being has been known to say, — "and between me
and it blazed up the fires of hell, I am so helpless
that I should still be forced to put out my hand and
take it."

What is this but demoniacal possession? What is
this but the undying worm and the quenchless flame,
self-introduced, self-kindled in the heart?

2. The second, and perhaps the commonest, condition
is that of *undecided struggle*. The man who has suffered the wild beast of the flesh to make its thick, car-
nivorous roar heard in his sanctuary — the youth who
has played lovingly with the glittering venomous impulse which shall soon break into a fiery flying serpent
— the man who, wilfully ceding to Satan the possession
even of an inch, has given to the Evil One a right and
a part within him, and forfeited his part in the Lord
Jesus Christ — that man has disturbed within him the
indefeasible autocracy of righteousness. He has rendered his task very perilous in the warfare which has
no discharge. It is infinitely easier to stand firm than
to restore a battle array which has once wavered and
been gored by inroads of the enemy. It is far easier
to win the battle than to check the rout. This was the
fatal experience depicted by St. Paul: "To will is present with me, but to do that which is good is not. So
the good which I would, I do not; but the evil which
I would not, that I practise. But if what I would not
that I do, it is no more I that do it, but sin that dwell-
eth in me. With the mind I serve the law of God; but
with the flesh the law of sin. Wretched man that I
am! who shall deliver me out of the body of this

death ? " (Rom. vii. 18–25.) It is the confession of Ovid : —

> " Video meliora, proboque
> Deteriora sequor." [1]

It is the exclamation of Louis XIV. : " I know those two men," when Massillon had been depicting the old man and the new man who exists within each one of us. All men must feel that though "the angel holds us by the hand," yet " the serpent has us by the heart." This explains the painful phenomenon of inconsistency. It accounts for the sudden frightful revelation of evil in the conduct of men who had passed for good. It accounts for the frequent phenomenon of sudden exposure and ruin in the case of men who, all their lives long, had seemed to be walking in the odor of sanctity. In many a man there are those *two* men, — the Adam and the Christ !

> " He seemed methought to live two lives in one,
> One busied still with matter to be done,
> While one apart sat on a sentry tower
> Watching the moral world."

And thus, in the quaint words of Tennyson : —

> "The piebald miscellany, man,
> Bursts of great heart, and slips in sensual mire."

3. The third condition alone represents the supreme of man, — the condition of settled victory in which a man, in armed and peaceful watchfulness, has achieved a secure and tranquil empire over himself by having attained the decisive victory over the passions of the

---

[1] Ovid, "Metamorphoses," vii.; cf. Euripides, "Medea," 1078 : —

> " καὶ μανθάνω μὲν οἷα δρᾶν μέλλω κακά
> θυμὸς δὲ κρείσσων τῶν ἐμῶν βουλευμάτων."

soul and the lusts of the body which are the signs of his moral affinity to the tiger and the ape. This is the condition of those whom in the Apocalypse St. John describes as the radiant company of the pure and undefiled, who, in white robes, and with palms in their hands, follow the Lamb whithersoever he goeth. These are they whom Plato describes as following the winged car of Zeus, and the twelve greater gods within the sphere of heaven, not like the rest which are lamed, and have their wings broken as they sink downwards through the violence of their chariot-steeds, and struggle and trample on one another.[1]

The poets, who are ever the greatest of our moral teachers, have constantly, and in all ages, dwelt on the happiness and glory of these victors over themselves.

So sings Virgil : —

> " Felix qui potuit rerum cognoscere caussas
> Quique metus omnes, et inexorabile fatum
> Subjecit pedibus, strepitumque Acherontis avari."

So Dante, to whom, as the reward of all his constancy and the issue of all his heart-shaking visions, Virgil says : —

> " Thy judgment is now free, correct, and sound,
> And thou wouldst err didst thou not do its bidding.
> I crown and mitre thee over thyself."[2]

So Shakespeare : —

> " I have lost the immortal part of myself, and what remains is
> bestial."

---

[1] Plato, "Phædrus," 246 E.
[2] Dante, "Purgatory," xxvii. 140–143 : "Perch io te sopra te corono e mitrio."

So Fletcher: —

> " Man is his own star; and the soul that can
> Render an honest and a perfect man,
> Commands all life, all influences, all fate,
> Nothing to him falls early, or too late:
> Our acts our angels are, or good or ill,
> Our fateful shadows that walk by us still."

So Sir Henry Wotton : —

> " How happy is he born or taught,
> That serveth not another's will,
> Whose armour is his honest thought,
> And simple truth his only skill;
> Whose passions not his masters are,
> Whose soul is still prepared for death,
> Untied unto the world by care
> Of public fame or private breath,
> This man is free from servile bands
> Of hope to rise, or fear to fall,
> Lord of himself, though not of lands,
> And having nothing, yet hath all."

So Milton, in prose : —

" He that holds himself in reverence and due esteem both for the dignity of God's image upon him and for the sign of His redemption which he thinks to be marked visibly upon his forehead, accounts himself a fit person to do the noblest and godliest deeds."

So Wordsworth, of the man —

> "Who, with a toward or untoward lot,
> Prosperous or adverse, to his wish or not,
> Plays, in the many games of life, that one
> Where what he most doth value must be won.
> This is the happy warrior; this is he
> Whom every man in arms would wish to be."

So Coleridge : —

> "Hath he not always treasures, always friends,
> The good great man? Three treasures — life, and light,
> And calm thoughts regular as infants' breath,

And three firm friends more sure than Day or Night—
Himself, his Maker, and the Angel Death."

So Matthew Arnold : —

"O air-born voice! long since, severely clear,
A cry like thine in mine own heart I hear, —
Resolve to be thyself; and know that he
Who finds himself loses his misery."

So Clough : —

"Seek seeker in thyself, and thou shalt find
In the stones bread, and life in the blank mind."

So Sir Lewis Morris : —

"Take thou no thought for aught save truth and right,
Content, if such thy fate, to die obscure;
Wealth palls, and honours, fame may not endure,
And noble souls soon weary of delight.
Live steadfastly. Be all a true man ought,
Let neither pleasures tempt, nor pain appal;
Who hath this he hath all things having nought,
Who hath it not hath nothing, having all."

And so another : —

"Be your own palace, or the world's your jail."

So Tennyson : —

"I envy not the beast that takes
His license in the fields of time,
Unfettered by the sense of crime,
To whom a conscience never wakes."

We may be quite sure beforehand that the first enunciation of a truth so striking and so necessary as this will be found in Scripture; and our Lord uttered it in the most concise yet pregnant form. In the Authorized Version the words read, " In your patience possess ye your souls " (Luke xxi. 19). But the word for " possess " is κτᾶσθαι; and the verse should be rendered, " In your patience ye shall win your souls." *Possession* of ourselves is not spontaneously bestowed upon us; it is a dominion which each man has to gain by labor and sore struggle.

And how is he to acquire it?

There is no answer but the old, old answer. A new answer, an original answer, would be a false one. The answer is best given in the pages of the old Book, ever old, yet ever new, which our mothers taught us. It is, "Watch and pray, lest ye enter into temptation." It is "Walk in the Spirit, and ye shall not fulfil the lusts of the flesh." The *body* of man may become frightfully depraved, — it may be turned from a sanctuary into a charnel-house, full of dead men's bones and all uncleanness; it may be desecrated from a shrine into a haunt of demons, the abode of goats and satyrs, and every obscene thing. The *soul* of man may be degraded from a home of noble virtues into a cage of unclean beasts. But the *spirit* of man can never be polluted. It may be grieved; it may be quenched; it may be stifled within us; but *perverted* it cannot be. For it is divine; it is eternal; it is God within us, and that whereby we have affinity with God. But the dove cannot fly in unclean places, nor can the Holy Spirit abide in a polluted heart. It requires thus a constant prayer, a constant effort, to keep the heart pure. St. Paul was "the man of the third heaven," the "heaven-treader," as the Greek Church calls him; yet even St. Paul says, "This one thing I do, forgetting those things that are behind, and stretching forth unto those things that are before, I press towards the mark of the prize of my high calling in Christ Jesus;" "so run I not as uncertainly; so fight I not as one who beateth the air [with hypocritic feints], but I blacken my body with blows [ὑπωπιάζω] and lead it about as a slave [δουλαγωγῶ], lest, by any means, after that I have preached to others, I myself should be rejected."

We see, then, that victory is only for the resolute and the brave. How long and how severely did the Greek wrestler and the Roman gladiator train themselves, as do the modern competitors in athletics at this day! How careful was their abstinence, how rigid their diet, how regular their exercises! If they could thus deny themselves, and control themselves, to win a corruptible crown, how much more should we do it to win the στέφανος ἀμαράντινος,[1] the crown woven of heaven's unfading amaranth? And it depends, under God, upon ourselves. "I confess it is my shame," says the weak debauchee in Othello, "but it is not in my virtue to amend it." "Virtue! a fig!" truly answers the resolute scoundrel. "'Tis in ourselves that we are thus and thus. Our bodies are gardens to the which our *wills* are gardeners; so that if we will plant nettles or sow lettuce, set hyssop and weed up thyme, supply it with one gender of herbs or distract it with many, either to have it sterile with idleness or manured with industry, why the power and corrigible authority of this lies in our *wills*. If the balance of our lives had not one scale of reason to poise another of sensuality, the blood and baseness of our natures would conduct us to most preposterous conclusions; but we have reason to cool our raging motions, our carnal stings, our unbitted lusts."

And let no young man say, "Alas! it is all too late! I have sold myself already, and for nought. I cannot dislodge from my enslaved soul the demons to whom, as

---

[1] 1 Pet. v. 4; κομιεῖσθε τὸν ἀμαράντινον τῆς δόξης στέφανον.

to strong men armed, I have betrayed the fortress. Almost as far as I can look back, even in days when the clearness of memory is lost in the mists of 'the dark backward and abysm of time,' I have been unfaithful. The crown has fallen from my head, for I have sinned." Let every youth indignantly expel these soft pleadings of despondency! They are snares of the Devil. Fight on, even if at sad moments it seems to you as though your fights were all defeats. Repentance, it has been said, is the younger brother of Innocence itself. Ah, how those two brothers differ! The elder brother, Innocence, is bright and strong and ruddy and beautiful and happy; the younger, Repentance, is pale, with withered features and downcast eyes and shaking hands. He often has to rescue a captive shut up in a lost self, that dungeon without iron bars, — a captive bound with fetters which are none the less heavy because they clank not and are invisible. But God who makes can remake, and who created can rescue. The task of Repentance is ten times harder than that of Innocence. It is ten times harder to break old habits, to recover lost ground, to rally the shamed and defeated soldiers of lost battles. Yet Repentance, by God's grace, has again and again won the most splendid victories in human lives. No *living* man is lost; while there is life there is hope. Sin is never a necessity, even when it has hardened into habit and petrified into character. Observe that Hope is a virtue as well as a grace. "Thou art wearied in the greatness of thy way. Yet saidst thou not, There is no hope." Had not St. Cyprian lived a thoroughly worldly and godless pagan life? Yet in middle age he became a saint of God, and underwent that transformation of character which he had deemed to be *impossible*. Had not St. Augustine lived through a corrupt boyhood, a sensual youth, an enslaved manhood ? yet did he not become "a new creation " ?

Not one of you is so fallen into evil as to be unredeemable. Christ, if you seek Him, if you rally every force within you to obey His will, Christ can restore your sight, can strengthen your palsy, can touch your leprous soul into pure health again. You are a sinner now, — tied and bound with the chain of your sins, — but Christ can roll off from you the strangling load and set you free, and you may yet die a holy man.

"Can it be true the hope he is declaring?
Oh, let us trust him, for his words are fair!
Man, what is this? and why art thou despairing?
God shall forgive thee all but thy despair."

There would be very much more to say on this great subject, but I conclude with one word on the supreme blessedness of self-conquest.

It may be measured by the shame and anguish of a disintegrated, a dual individuality, a reed shaken by the wind, a life swayed hither and thither by opposing influence, a character composed of : —

"Pulses of nobleness, and aches of shame."

To the undecided and the defeated, God has given their hearts' desire, and sent leanness withal into their souls. They have plucked Dead Sea apples and are poisoned ; they have clutched at bubbles which have burst at their touch. Old age leaves them like a boat which has struck upon a bank of mud in a fast-ebbing tide, which for them can flow no more. Their bodies are their prison-house. Their self-poisoned self clings to them like a Nessus-shirt of agony which they think that they can never tear off. Such a man carries about with him, wherever he goes, his own punishment forever. Which way he flies is hell; himself is hell. He is, as one said who knew what it meant by grim experience : —

"Lord of himself, that heritage of woe."

On the other hand, he who has attained to self-mastery " has his own self for a better possession and an abiding." The old copyists failed to understand the depth and grandeur of that passage of the Epistle to the Hebrews (Heb. x. 34). They altered it into a meaning, true indeed, but much less profound and original, by writing, as in our Authorized Version, " knowing *in yourselves* [ἐν ἑαυτοῖς] that ye have *in heaven* a better and an enduring substance." The text and version are trebly faulty. The verse really consoles the suffering Hebrews in the midst of poverty and persecution, and accounts for their joy amid it all, by saying that they exulted in mercy and good works, " learning [by these very trials] to recognize that *ye had your own selves for a better possession* " than all the earthly goods of which they had been spoiled, and an *abiding* possession of which neither earth nor hell could ever rob them. That possession is the spiritual, the eternal life, overarched by the inward azure of that peace which no earthly clouds can darken. Even a heathen could feel *something* of this dignity. In one of Seneca's tragedies an aged attendant is pointing out to Medea the hopelessness of her fortunes : —

" Abiere Colchi, conjugis nulla est fides;
Nihilque superest, opibus e tantis, tibi," —

" Your husband is faithless; your soldiers have gone;
your wealth is scattered; what remains to you?" — "*Medea superest*," " Medea still remains to me!" is the magnificent reply. I am still *myself*. He who has mastered
himself stands on the sunlit hills above the storms.
Fortune can strip him of all outward resources, but not
of himself, not of the unconquerable will. The tree is
still a tree, with all the potentialities of life within it,
though the whirlwind have stripped away its leaves.

" Old age hath yet his honour and his toil:
Death closes all; but something ere the end,
Some work of noble note, may yet be done."

Therefore let every youth aim, first of all, and most
of all, at self-mastery. Without it, he must be base
and miserable ; with it, he cannot but be happy. Without it, other things are but " gifts of the evil genii
which are curses in disguise." With it, he is God's
child, the possessor of blessedness now, the heir of
eternal happiness hereafter. Without it he will have
nothing to give back to the God who made him but
shame and abject ruin; with it, he has fulfilled the
highest ends of his being, and shall have life for
evermore.